# Thought Bubbles,

## A Collection of Cartoons

by jbro

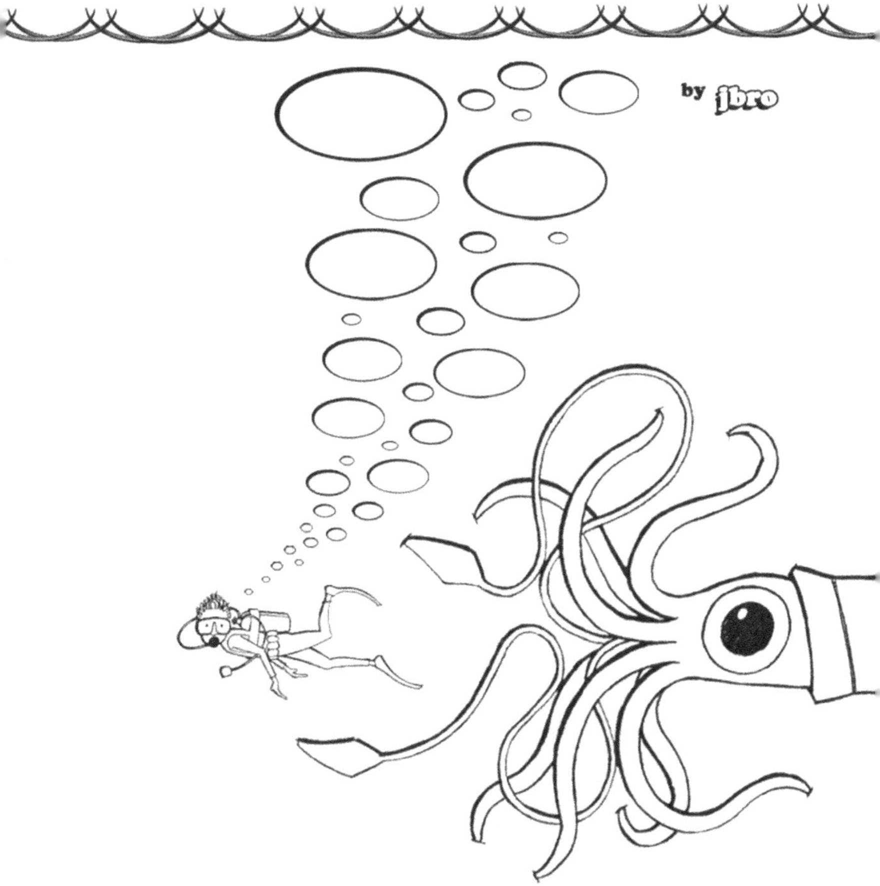

ISBN:  979-8-218-04645-3  (paperback)
ISBN:  979-8-218-04087-1  (ebook)

*...to all the dogs I've loved before.*

# Contents

AQUA · TICKS
(AQUATICS)

IN TOTO

MIDEVIL MAXIMS

DECOMPOSER

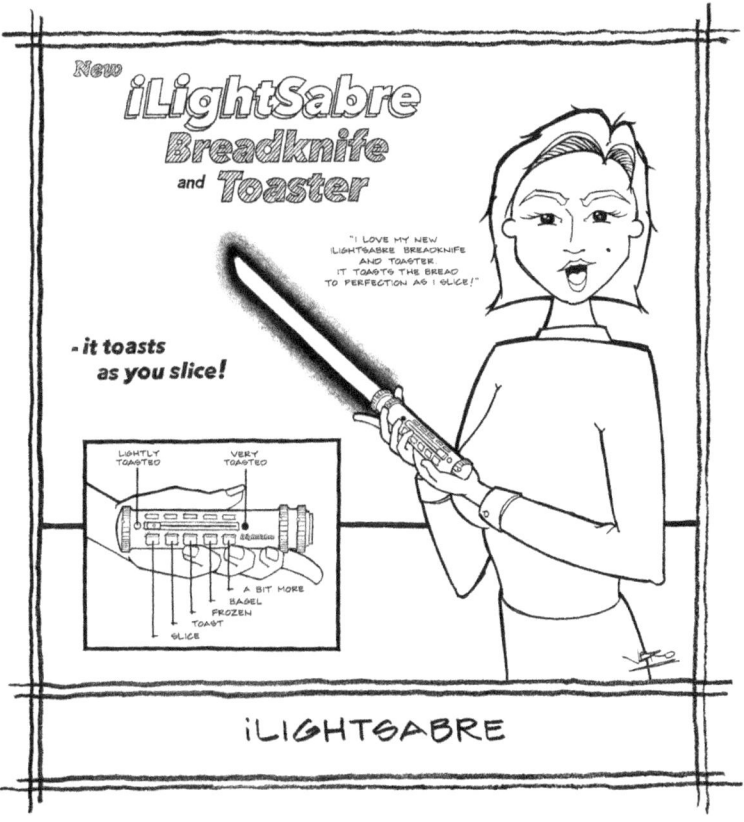

BOOTY

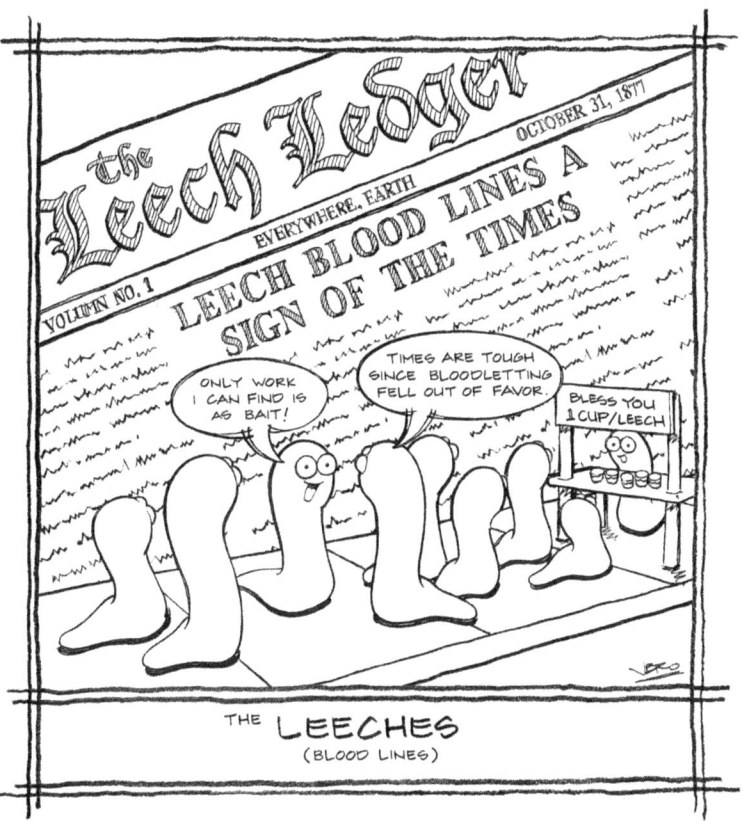

THE LEECHES
(BLOOD LINES)

ABDOMINAL SNOWMAN

XOXO's

THE **MAGNATOR**

XOXO'S

THE MAGNATOR

HOME THEATER

BUNG

BON APPÉTIT

AQUA · TICKS
(BLOOD IN THE WATER)

HOLE

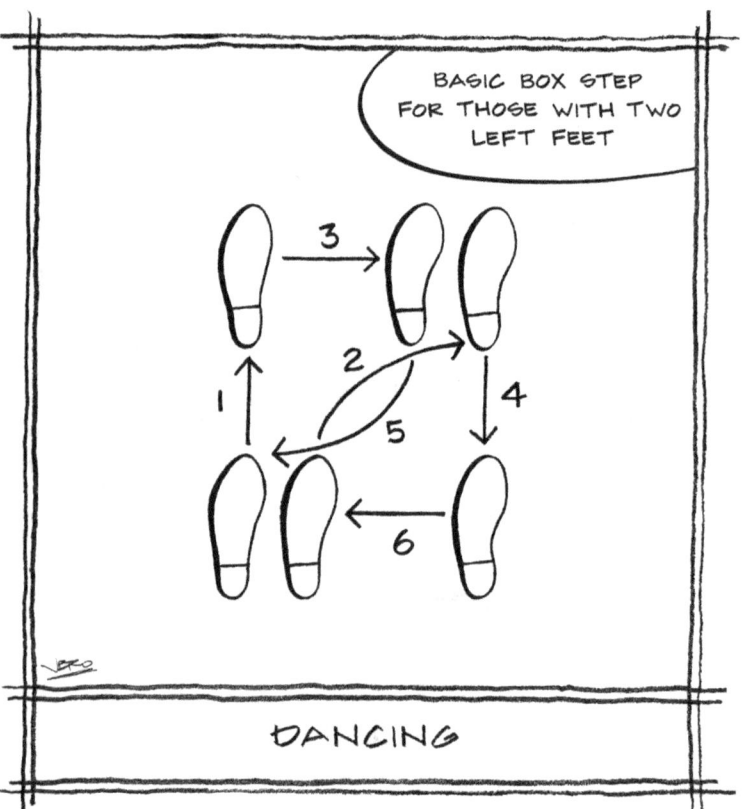

FLEA MARKET

DENUDE

FILL IN THE BLANK

OH CRAP

## THE TREBUCHET MAGNATOR

CAT'S PAJAMAS

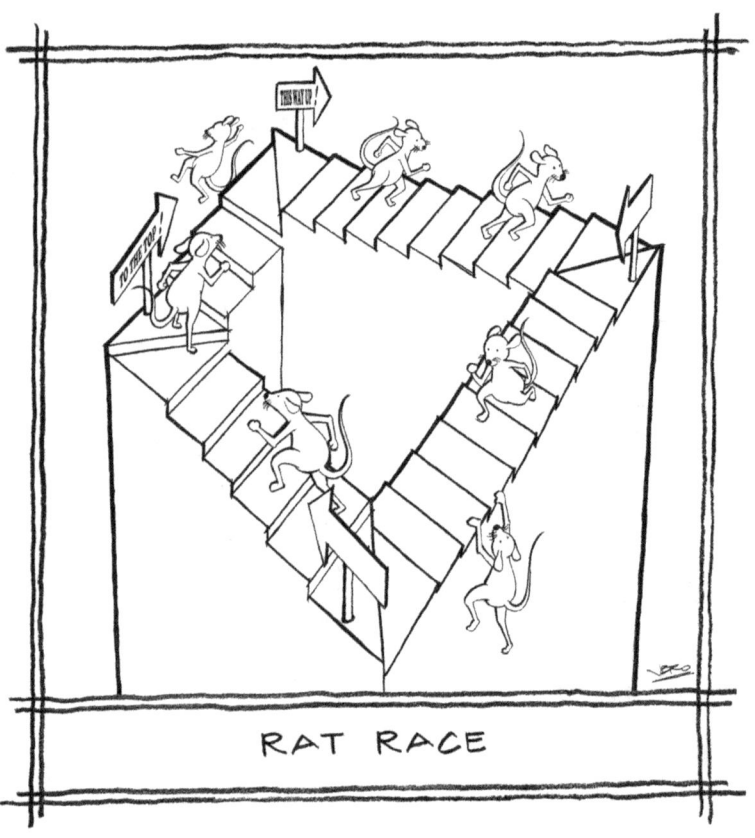

RAT RACE

AQUA · TICKS
(LOST HEAD)

BUSTED

CI(R)CADIAN RHYHMS

CEREAL KILLER

LUCKY

THE **LEECHES**
( LEECH LORE )

LEFT BRAINED

DESTINATION

DUET

THE STICKY BATTLE MATTE

AQUA·TICKS
(VAMPIRE)

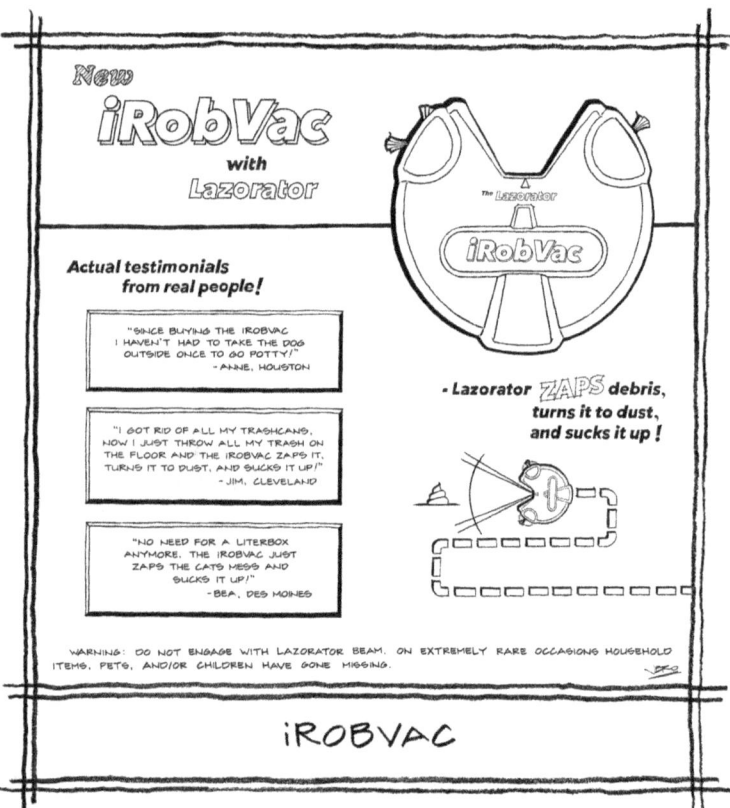

**New**

# iRobVac

**with Lazorator**

**Actual testimonials from real people!**

"SINCE BUYING THE IROBVAC I HAVEN'T HAD TO TAKE THE DOG OUTSIDE ONCE TO GO POTTY!"
- ANNE, HOUSTON

"I GOT RID OF ALL MY TRASHCANS, NOW I JUST THROW ALL MY TRASH ON THE FLOOR AND THE IROBVAC ZAPS IT, TURNS IT TO DUST, AND SUCKS IT UP!"
- JIM, CLEVELAND

"NO NEED FOR A LITERBOX ANYMORE. THE IROBVAC JUST ZAPS THE CATS MESS AND SUCKS IT UP!"
- BEA, DES MOINES

**- Lazorator ZAPS debris, turns it to dust, and sucks it up!**

WARNING: DO NOT ENGAGE WITH LAZORATOR BEAM. ON EXTREMELY RARE OCCASIONS HOUSEHOLD ITEMS, PETS, AND/OR CHILDREN HAVE GONE MISSING.

iROBVAC

MOCKINGBIRDS

VESPADRILLS

S.C.U.A.
(SPORTS CLICHÉ USERS ANONYMOUS)

LUNCH

OFF-SITE

SNAKE EYES

HOT AIR

CONFESSION

AUNTEATER

YAK

ALL ABORDT

DAY OFF

OH DEER

## THE PUTRID ODAIRE WAFTAIRE

BREADCRUMBS

FLEABAG

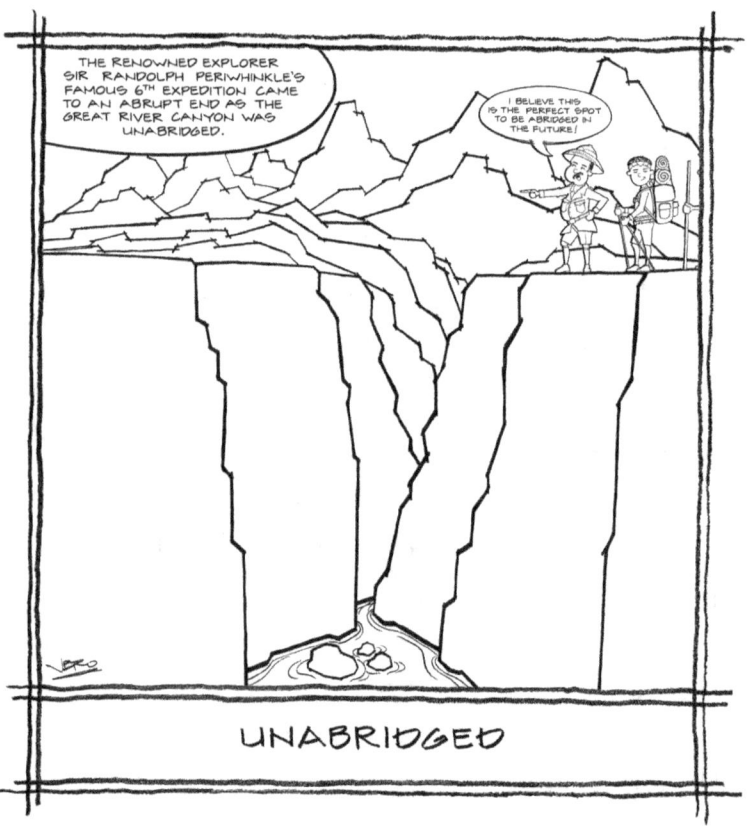

UNABRIDGED

BIG FOOT

# AIR TRAVEL

THE **LEECHES**

(LEECH LEGENDS LANE)

ONE ARM BANDIT

PARASITE PLAZA